AIRDRIE

DEEP FOREST

START AND
FINISH LINE

RACE COURSE

Copyright © 2009 by Verlagshaus Jacoby & Stuart, Berlin, Germany
English translation copyright © 2011 by Shelley Tanaka
First published in German as *Hund & Hase* by Jacoby & Stuart
First published in English in Canada and the USA in 2011 by Groundwood Books

Groundwood Books / House of Anansi Press
110 Spadina Avenue, Suite 801, Toronto, Ontario M5V 2K4
or c/o Publishers Group West
1700 Fourth Street, Berkeley, CA 94710

We acknowledge for their financial support of our publishing program the
Government of Canada through the Canada Book Fund (CBF).

Library and Archives Canada Cataloguing in Publication
Berner, Rotraut Susanne
Hound and hare / Rotraut Susanne Berner ; translated by
Shelley Tanaka.
Translation of: Hund und Hase.
ISBN 978-0-88899-987-0
I. Tanaka, Shelley II. Title.
PZ10.3.B464Ho 2011   j833   C2010-905902-6

The illustrations are in color pencil and ink.
Printed and bound in China

Rotraut Susanne Berner

HOUND AND HARE

Translated by Shelley Tanaka

Groundwood Books
House of Anansi Press
Toronto Berkeley

1 Harley and Hugo

This is a story about Harley Hare and Hugo Hound. They live in Great Bone, a little village beside a river.

Harley and Hugo see each other at school every day.
They are interested in the same things.

Even so, they never say a word to each other.

Why? Because the Hare and Hound families can't
stand one another.

There is an age-old custom in Great Bone.

Every Monday, Wednesday and Friday, the Hound family goes to the house where the Hare family lives. They stand near the house and sing mean songs with bad rhymes.

> "Rabbit feet and rabbit stew,
> That's all hares are good for, too!"

Or,
      "Hares are always twitching noses,
        Got big feet with funny toeses!"
And so it goes, all day long, right up until dark.

And what happens every Tuesday, Thursday and Saturday?

The Hare family meets in front of the Hound family's house to pay them back.

"It's a dog-eat-dog world,
It's a dog-eat-dog world,
It's a dog-eat-dog world..."

Or,

> "Hounds just bay at the full moon,
> Hope you leave our village soon!"

And on and on it goes, right up until dinnertime.
Sunday is their day off. On Sunday things are quiet.
And today is Sunday. It's a hot one, too. The dog days
of summer, you might say.

"Why can't I go to the field and race with the others?" asks Harley.

"Because," says Mrs. Hare. "It's too dangerous. Those Hounds will be there, and you know what that means. Why not play with your little brother instead?"

"Everyone is going to the Big Race this afternoon. Why do I have to stay home?" asks Hugo.

"Because," says Mrs. Hound. "We want to stay away from those carrot munchers. You are better off here looking after your little sister!"

"But there's a prize for the winner," Harley says.
"You're mean."

"Don't get your whiskers in a twist," says Father. "Just remember one thing. Hares don't run with hounds."

"But I want to run in the race," says Hugo.

"Forget it," says Father. "You don't want to spend time with those flat-footed lettuce nibblers."

"Have you ever tried to make friends with a hound?"
asks Harley.

"Good grief, no!" says Auntie. "But your great-great-grandfather knew one once. And if you know one, you know them all. Dog-gone flea scratchers!"

"So why don't we like the Hares, exactly?" asks Hugo.

"It's a long story," sighs Grandfather. "Nobody quite knows how it started. But it doesn't matter. Hares are nosy, and they have too many children."

"This place is going to the dogs," Harley sighs. "There's no one to play with. They're all at the Big Race. I'm the only

one left behind, stuck here like a pooch in a pup tent."

"I'll turn into an old dog before anything happens here," mutters Hugo.

"Am I just going to lie around like a scared little bunny? Let's hop to it!"

And so it happens.

Paws pop out the window, fly over the fence and
scurry down the street to the edge of town.

On the meadow, excitement is building. The race is about to begin.

That's when Hugo and Harley finally reach the starting line.

"It's about time!" calls Rudy Raven. "This is a race, not a bunny hop. Get in line, you two."

"Dognapping again?" grumbles Hana Hen as she gives Hugo his number.

Rudy gives the signal.
"On your marks. Get set. Go!"

And they're off. Harley Hare, Hugo Hound, Cathy Cat, Dana Doe, Billy Boar, Gavin Goat, Ronnie Raccoon, Freddy Fox, Bobby Badger and Sherry Sheep.

They thunder down the field. Everyone cheers.

Up in her high chair, Olivia Owl can see everything.
"Ladies and gentlemen, the Big Race has begun! Hugo
Hound and Harley Hare are in the lead. Gavin Goat and

Billy Boar are right behind them. But we are worried about the weather. Will someone win the race before the storm breaks? Stay tuned for the latest update."

3 The Storm

Hugo and Harley already have a big lead.

"You hare-brained furball!" shouts Hugo. "Get out of my way!"

"You're nothing but a hound dog!" cries Harley. "I'll show you!"

"Bone chomper!"
"Bossy bunny!"

The race is half over. Howard Hedgehog reports. "Breaking news! Hugo Hound and Harley Hare are running faster than the wind! Freddy Fox is right behind

them! But the first drops have started to fall. Soon it will be raining like hares and dogs!"

The wind is blowing. Olivia Owl can barely hang on to her seat.

"Ladies and gentlemen," she says. "I'm afraid the race must be stopped due to the storm. And here is an important announcement. Pippa Pig is missing. If you find her, please bring her to the main tent."

But Hugo and Harley just run and run. Wet and dripping, farther and farther.

Then lightning strikes nearby.
"Hugo, stop!" Harley cries. "It's too dangerous!"

Hugo comes to a clearing. He stops under a big tree.

"Don't stand there!" cries Harley. "Lightning can strike the tree. I know what to do in a storm. Come on!"

"Mommy," sobs Hugo. "Help! I'm scared!"
"Don't be afraid," says Harley. "The storm will
stop soon."

Harley is right. The storm passes.
Night comes. It is very quiet and very dark.
"But where are we?" asks Hugo.

4 Lost!

The radio reports that Hugo Hound, Harley Hare and
Pippa Pig are missing.

"Oh, dear!" says Auntie. "Poor Harley! He has not even
had his dinner!"

On the evening news everyone is asked to come to the main tent to help search.

"My poor baby," moans Mrs. Hound. "Hugo is so afraid of storms! What if he catches cold?"

"Mommy," cries Harley. "I'm lost! Why didn't I listen to you? We will never get back home!"

"Chin up," says Hugo. "I know what to do. Follow me. You'll see, we'll soon find our way."

Hugo is right. There is the road, right in front of them.
"That's Bobby Badger's house!" cries Hugo. "If we turn
left we will come to the bridge over the river."

"Shhh," whispers Harley. "Do you hear something?"

"Look!" cries Hugo. "Someone is sitting under that tree.
The rain has flooded the meadow!"

"It's Pippa!" Harley says. "Shall we dog paddle?"
And they both pull off their shoes and jump into
the water.

And so little Pippa is safe, thanks to good teamwork.

At last they reach the road. They are soaked to the bone and dog-tired.

"I'm so hungry," Hugo says. "What I wouldn't give for a dish of rabbit stew!"

"If only I had my cozy houndstooth jacket," says Harley. "I'm shivering all over."

"I want my daddy!" wails Pippa.

When Hugo, Harley and Pippa walk into the big tent, everyone cheers. No one is happier than Pippa's father, Percy.

He takes little Pippa in his arms, and everyone agrees
that Hugo and Harley deserve a reward.

"We have made a decision," says Rudy Raven. "Hugo and Harley will share first prize for the winner of the Big Race!"

He brings in a large box. The crowd is very quiet.
Then Hugo and Harley lift the lid together.

It's a pair of rollerskates! Brand spanking new yellow rollerskates.

One rollerskate for Harley.
And one for Hugo.

Now there is a new custom in Great Bone.

Every Monday, Wednesday and Friday, Harley Hare puts on the brand spanking new yellow rollerskates. He skates back and forth in front of his house. Hour after hour, until it gets dark.

And every Tuesday, Thursday and Saturday, Hugo
Hound puts on the brand spanking new yellow rollerskates.

Then he glides up and down the path to his house.
Over and over, until it is time for dinner.

On Sunday, they take the day off.

Or, sometimes, they go for a skate together.

Other books by
Rotraut Susanne Berner

Definitely Not for Little Ones: Some Very Grimm
Fairy-Tale Comics

The Winter Book